The Fastest Quitter In Town

Whenever things don't go right for Johnny Colmer in a baseball game, he can't help yelling, "I quit!" Pretty soon the boys don't want him on their team.

One day, Johnny's great-grandfather loses a treasured ring that was given to him many years ago by his wife. Everyone looks for a while but finally gives up—everyone, that is, except Johnny.

This story tells about a boy who, through his love for his great-grandfather, learns the importance of not quitting on himself.

The FASTEST QUITTER in TOWN

by **phyllis green**

illustrations by
lorenzo lynch

young scott books

Published by Young Scott Books, a Division of the
Addison-Wesley Publishing Co., Inc., Reading, Mass. 01867.

Library of Congress Cataloging in Publication Data

Green, Phyllis.
The fastest quitter in town.

SUMMARY: Because Johnny knows the importance of
the lost ring to his grandfather he keeps searching for
it and learns the value of not giving up.
I. Lynch, Lorenzo, 1932-   illus.   II. Title.
PZ7.G82615Fas   [Fic]   72-761
ISBN 0-201-09170-4

For *Bob, Sharon, and Bruce*

The pitcher began the wind-up.
He threw the ball to home plate.
Crack! The batter hit a grounder.
The shortstop scooped it up.
He threw it to Johnny Colmer.

"Easy out, Johnny," he yelled.
Johnny touched one foot on first base,
ready to make the catch.
He knew he had it!

But the only thing he caught was . . . air!

Johnny threw down his mitt. "I quit," he said.
Everybody started yelling.
"You always quit when you do something stupid!"
"Why don't you learn to catch?
Then you won't quit so much."

Johnny yelled back. "I *can* catch.
Old Gromering can't throw."

"Come on. Let's play without him.
We don't need him," the boys said.

Johnny picked up his mitt and ran off the field.
When he got to the edge of the schoolyard,
he sat down on the curb.

Tears made paths down his dusty cheeks.
He felt awful.
He had promised himself that
he would play the whole game today.
But he had quit right at the start.
If only he had been chosen for the other team.
If only old Gromering knew how to throw a ball.

Johnny got up and wiped his face on his shirt.
They would never let him back in the game.
He decided to go see Great-Grandfather and
tell him about Gromering's bad throw.
Johnny Colmer lived with his parents
at 1206 Fifth Street.
His grandparents lived next door.

But someone else lived there, too—
Johnny's great-grandfather.
Johnny's great-grandfather was ninety!
Great-Grandfather's eyes had become very bad.
He could hardly see anything.
But he had lots of good stories to tell.
He told Johnny about the first automobiles,
and about days when there was no television
and how nobody talked in the first movies.

When Johnny arrived,
the first thing Great-Grandfather said was,
"Short game today?"

Johnny put his hands in his pockets.
He didn't say anything.

"I thought you were going to play
the whole game today. Something go wrong?"
asked Great-Grandfather.

"Yeah," said Johnny.

"I see," Great-Grandfather said. "Well, do you
suppose your grandmother has any cookies
hidden away from us?"

It was hard for Great-Grandfather to get up,
but Johnny helped him.

He got the cookies from the top
of the refrigerator.
"Fig newtons," he said.

"Oh, no!" said Great-Grandfather.
"They aren't cookies. They're just bitter medicine."

"I like them," Johnny said.

"Well, don't save any for me. I'd rather sit here
and starve to death," said Great-Grandfather.
Johnny ate five fig newtons.

"Get yourself some milk," Great-Grandfather said.
"Then tell me about today. Someone break the rules?"

"No," Johnny said. "Just Joe Gromering.
He thinks he's so hot.
Only he never learned to throw a ball."

"That so?" said his great-grandfather.
"He's that bad, huh?"

"He's not *real* bad. Just throws a little high."
"For you."
"Yeah."

"That's why you quit? You missed the ball?"

"Not exactly. I mean, kind of.
Well, tomorrow I'm going to play the whole game
no matter what those stupid guys do."

Great-Grandfather patted his shoulder.
"Tomorrow you'll be ready for him.
Tomorrow you'll catch the ball.
But Johnny, if by some chance you miss it,
don't give up. Keep playing. It's a game.
You're supposed to have fun."

The next afternoon Johnny took his mitt.
He walked over to the schoolyard.
"Oh no," the boys groaned. "Here comes Colmer,
the fastest quitter in town."

Johnny stood around just hitting his mitt
while the other boys played.

Finally one boy called, "All right, Colmer.
We'll give you one more chance.
Are you going to play the whole game today?"

"Yeah," said Johnny.

"O.K. Get out in left field."

In the third inning, when Johnny went to bat,
he hit the ball far into center field.
It looked like a homer.
He ran fast. As he turned third base,
he saw the ball moving toward the catcher.

"SLIDE!" someone yelled.
He SLID!

He got up smiling and brushed the dirt
off his torn pants.
He was sure he was safe by a hair.

"Out!" yelled everyone.

"I'm safe!" Johnny shouted.

"You're out!" they yelled.

Johnny tried not to say anything,
but suddenly the words came out.
"I quit."

Everybody began to scream and yell.
"That was your last chance, Colmer.
You're off the team for good.
Don't come around ever again," they said.

Johnny went straight to see Great-Grandfather.
But he didn't tell him about the game
because the old man was very upset.
"What's the matter, Great-Grandpa?" Johnny asked.

"Oh, Johnny," the old man said, "thank goodness
you've come. I need your eyes, Johnny.
You know my ring, the gold one
with the real diamond in the center?
The one my dear Nancy gave me?
You poor child, you never knew her.
She died before you were born.
She's your great-grandmother, Johnny.
And I've lost the ring she gave me."

"Where did you lose it, Great-Grandpa?
I'll find it," said Johnny.

Johnny crawled under Great-Grandfather's bed.
He pulled up the pillow on his favorite chair.
He put his fingers in the cracks to see
if the ring had fallen in there.
He looked through Great-Grandfather's pillowcase
and sheets and blankets to see if the ring
had fallen off his finger while he slept.
He looked everywhere and Great-Grandfather
encouraged him.

"Look in the window seat, Johnny,
and under the rug, and on the television table.
It was just a small diamond but it was real.
A genuine diamond and Nancy gave it to me."

But Johnny couldn't find it.

Johnny looked for the ring again the next day.
He looked every day for a week.
But he did not find the ring.

"I've got to find that ring, Johnny.
I promised I'd never take it off.
And now I've lost it."

"It's not your fault," Johnny said.
"It must have fallen off.
You can't help that."

"But what will Nancy think?"
The old man was crying.

Each day the old man got more disturbed.
He fussed a lot and cried a lot.
Johnny's parents were very worried.

One day Mrs. Colmer had an idea.
"I saw a ring just like his at the 5 & 10,
and I bought it," she said.
"Johnny, you give it to him
and tell him it's his ring.
He'll never know.
He can't see anything any more."

"But I can't," Johnny said.
"He will know! He's not stupid.
He wants the ring with the real diamond in it."

"Johnny, if we thought it would help,
we would *buy* him a good ring
with a little diamond in it.
But he's a very old man.
He forgets easily.
He would probably lose it, too."

"O.K.," Johnny said, "but I just know that
he'll know it isn't his ring."

Johnny went to see Great-Grandfather.
He closed the door to the room so no one would hear.
He put the ring in Great-Grandfather's hand.

"Johnny," he said, "that's not my ring."

"I know, Great-Grandpa. But I want you to pretend.
Can you pretend?
Mom and Dad and Grandma and Grandpa are all upset
because you're upset over losing the diamond ring.
They want you to think this is your ring
and to be happy again.
Can you pretend it's your ring? Please!
And I promise if your ring can be found,
I will find it.
I will never stop looking. I will never give up."

"Do you mean that, Johnny?
Do you mean you won't quit on me?
O.K. Johnny. You're my buddy. I'll pretend."

For almost a month, Johnny didn't go near the
schoolyard when the boys were playing ball.
He was busy with his promise to Great-Grandfather.
He looked and looked.
Each day when he woke up he always felt it would be
the special day when he would find the ring.
But it never was.

One day when Johnny went to see Great-Grandfather,
the old man said, "Johnny, I feel like a little sun.
Help me out to the porch, will you?"

"You haven't been out for a long time, Great-Grandpa."

"Well, when you get old, you'll find out, Johnny,
it's just easier to stay inside
on your favorite chair and snooze."

They sat on the porch together.
The sun felt good on the old man's wrinkled hands.
He rubbed the warmth into them.
He touched the 5 & 10 Cent Store ring.
"You haven't stopped looking, have you, Johnny?
"I can't keep pretending. I've got to have that ring."

"Great-Grandpa, don't give up on me. I'll find it.
Really, I'll find it!
Just don't quit on me, Great-Grandpa."

Johnny looked at the backyard.
"Great-Grandpa, were you out back here
on the day you lost your ring?"

The old man bent his head to one side.
"I don't know.
It's so hard to remember any more."

"Maybe you were. I've looked everywhere else."
Johnny got down and crawled around the grass.
He felt through the thick blades with his fingers.

Great-Grandfather got excited.
"Johnny, sometimes when I'm out here,
I walk over to the rock garden to touch
the marigolds and zinnias.
I can't see them too well, but I like to touch them
and know they're there.

Look over there, Johnny.
I've got a feeling.
I've got a good feeling, Johnny."

Johnny crawled through the grass looking, looking.
He came to the rock garden.
He parted the marigolds and touched the earth
around their stems.
He felt around the edges of the rocks.

He separated the red and yellow zinnias and
looked through their leaves.
He saw something near a zinnia stem—something shiny.
"Oh please let it be the ring," thought Johnny.
Something gold sparkled in the sunlight.

"Great-Grandpa!" he yelled. "I found it!"
He took the ring to his great-grandfather.

Tears came to the old man's eyes.
He felt the lost ring.
There was dirt caked on the little diamond.

"Dear God, he found my ring.
Johnny found my diamond ring.
Thank you, Johnny. I don't know
what I would have done without you."

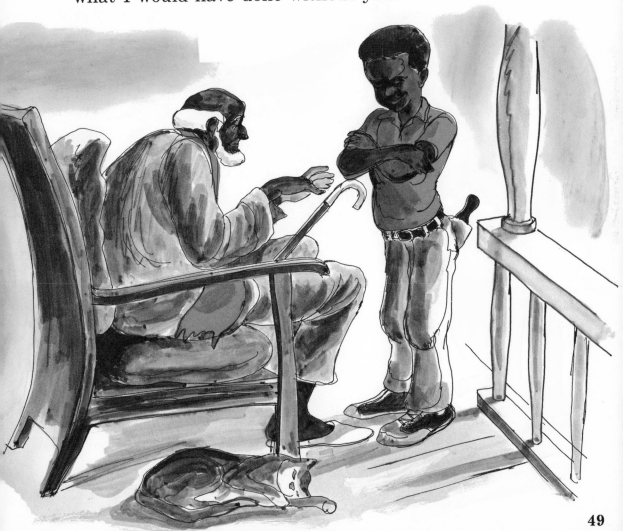

The whole family was thrilled.
Johnny's grandmother put tape around the ring.
Now it would fit Great-Grandfather's finger better
and not fall off again.
And Johnny felt so good inside.
It was such a good feeling to have found the ring.
He hadn't given up.
He hadn't even wanted to quit.
The ring was so important to Great-Grandfather,
he *never* would have quit.

The next day he went around to the schoolyard.
The boys all laughed when they saw him.
"Well, look who's here," they said.
"Long time, no see."

"How about one more chance?" Johnny asked.

The boys hooted and laughed.
"For somebody who doesn't know a strike from a ball?
For Colmer, the quitter?" they said.

Johnny smiled.
"For Colmer, the fastest hitter in town," he said.

The boy at bat called, "I vote no on the quitter.
He was kicked out for good."
Other boys shouted, "No! He's a quitter."

But Gromering yelled, "C'mon, you guys.
You know we need another player.
Get over on third base, Johnny."

Johnny ran to third
before they could change their minds.

It was after supper when he dropped in
to see Great-Grandfather.
"Where have you been, Johnny?
You're so late today. I thought you forgot about me."

"I was playing ball," said Johnny.

"It's awful late. We've had dinner already,"
Great-Grandfather said.

"Yeah. I was late for dinner at home too,
but Mom warmed it up for me.
Can't you guess why I'm late, Great-Grandpa?"

"Well, let's see," Great-Grandfather said,
trying to remember.

"Great-Grandpa, I used to be a quitter!
But today I didn't quit. And I feel great."

"You a quitter?" Great-Grandfather asked.
"That doesn't seem possible. Not my Johnny.
Well, it's so hard to remember any more.
Let's go get some cookies."

Johnny helped the old man into the kitchen.
They ate the chocolate chip cookies
that Johnny's grandmother had made that day.

Great-Grandfather said, "It's late.
You came late today.
Where have you been?"

Johnny looked at his great-grandfather.
He reached over and touched the lines
in the old man's face.
They were so deep.
They kept getting deeper and deeper.
"I was playing baseball, Great-Grandpa."

"Did you win? I sure hope you won, Johnny."

"No, we lost," Johnny said.
"Boy, did we ever lose!
Twenty to seven. But I got two home runs!
I don't know what the team would
have done without me."

"I wish I could have seen you make those home runs.
Well, I'm so tired. I better get to bed,"
Great-Grandfather said.

Johnny helped him back to his room.
"Goodnight, Great-Grandpa," Johnny said.
He kissed his forehead.
"And thanks. Thanks a lot."
"Don't thank me," Great-Grandfather said.
"Your grandmother made the cookies.
See you tomorrow."

About the Author

PHYLLIS GREEN has published poetry, articles, and fiction in national magazines. In 1971 she was staffing co-chairman of the Oakland University Creative Writing Conference, having formerly been a pupil of Lawrence Hart and a member of his poetry seminar in San Rafael, California.

She has a master's degree in education from the University of Pittsburgh. Her work experiences have ranged from third-grade teacher and special education teacher for mentally retarded children to band vocalist and summer theater actress.

Mrs. Green lives in Livonia, Michigan, with her husband and their son and daughter.

About the Artist

LORENZO LYNCH has illustrated two children's books, one of which, *The Hot Dog Man,* he also wrote. He grew up in Alabama and came to New York to study illustrating and advertising art at the Art Students League and at the School of Visual Arts. He now has his own art and design studio and teaches art techniques to school children part-time.

Mr. Lynch says, *"The Fastest Quitter in Town* deals with members of our society who are usually pushed aside and ignored—the very old and the young. The compassion and dependency between the great-grandfather and the boy remind me of my childhood relationship with my own grandfather."

Mr. Lynch, his wife, and five children live in Brooklyn.